ISBN-13: 978 - 1987643107
ISBN-10: 1987643100

Printed in the U.S.A.

The edition first printing, April, 2018

Murph is a happy snail.

He lives in a garden in Maine. He eats plants,
and lives a good snaily life.

Murph liked to explore all of the plants in the garden.

On Murph's birthday he made a wish.

On his way out of the garden, Murph made friends with a ladybug.

At the edge of the garden was a forest.

It was full of mushrooms.

Murph loved to crawl on mushrooms.

He also enjoyed just hanging around.

Murph wandered through the forest to see what he could find.

In the forest he found a fairy house.

He knocked but nobody was home.

Murph met a turtle friend in the woods.

You look ancient!

I'm 100 years old.

He gave him a ride to the base of the mountain.

It took a long time but Murph
crawled up the mountain.

At the top, he stopped to admire the view.

By the time he got back down, he was thirsty. So he stopped to take a drink from the lake at the bottom.

After he was done drinking he looked around and realized that the leaves were changing. It was fall!

Look what
I can do!

Murph found a
pumpkin to carve.
It took him awhile
because he had to
chew it out.
He was very proud
of it when he was
done.

For a little while on his journey,
Murph became a pirate.

But he missed the feeling of dirt under his shell. When he got back to land, he saw it was snow covered. Murph built a snowman and called him Stu.

Murph liked to play Santa and give gifts
to all the snaily children.

Murph also liked
to trim the tree.

Murph discovered that it's too cold this winter for him to go back to his garden.

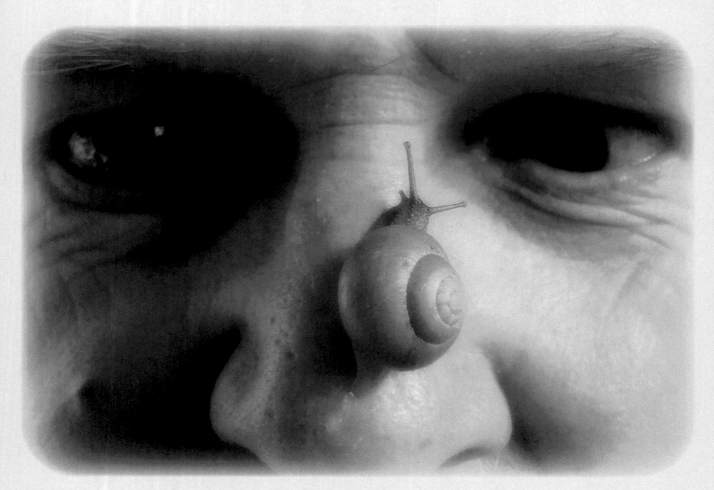

He is invited to stay with some human friends that he had met until springtime.

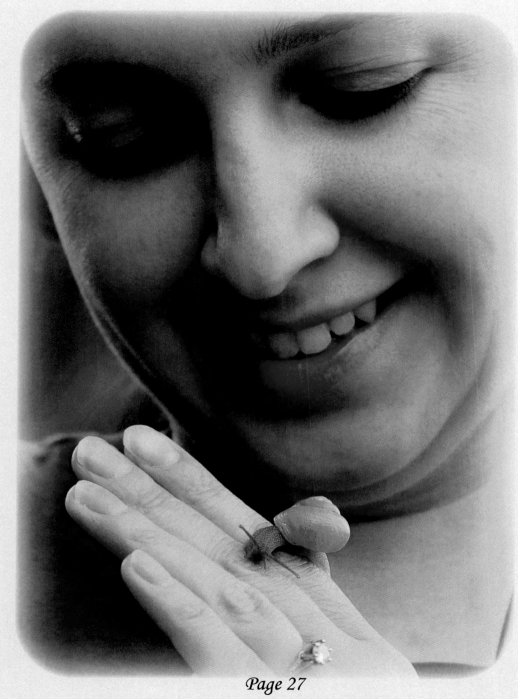

Murph was given his very own mug to drink from!

"MURPH"

His favorite beverage was hot cocoa.

Murph even got into rock painting.

When he left in the springtime,
he thanked them for their kindness.
He noticed they had a hummingbird feeder and
made another new friend.

The hummingbird offered to fly Murph back
home after they ate.

When Murph got back to his garden,
it was almost his birthday again!

He thought back to everything that happened in the past year. He had made all the adventures that he'd wished for come true. And now he was back home in the garden that he loves.
And he is happy.

About the Authors

Don is a self-taught photographer with a passion for wildlife and scenery. He had always been drawn to the beauty of the natural world, from the intimate details to the grand scenes.
He is a freelance photographer and the owner and operator of Eastern Maine Images, a gallery and gift shop located in Eastport Maine.
Kathleen works a day job as a registered dental hygienist at a health center. She spent a lot of her childhood in the local library and finds it very fulfilling to work on this literary project with her husband.
Murph is their pet snail who resides in a ten gallon tank in their living room. He loves lettuce and being in the spotlight.

Made in the USA
Monee, IL
17 September 2020